The Taming of the Shrew

Sweet Cherry
Publishing

Published by Sweet Cherry Publishing Limited
Unit E, Vulcan Business Complex,
Vulcan Road,
Leicester, LE5 3EB,
United Kingdom

First published in the USA in 2013
ISBN: 978-1-78226-084-4

©Macaw Books

Title: The Taming of the Shrew
North American Edition

Text & Illustration by Macaw Books 2013

www.sweetcherrypublishing.com

Printed and bound by Wai Man Book Binding (China) Ltd. Kowloon, H.K.

About Shakespeare

William Shakespeare, regarded as the greatest writer in the English language, was born in Stratford-upon-Avon in Warwickshire, England (around April 23, 1564). He was the third of eight children born to John and Mary Shakespeare.

Shakespeare was a poet, playwright, and dramatist. He is often known as England's national poet and the "Bard of Avon." Thirty-eight plays, 154 sonnets, two long narrative poems, and several other poems are attributed to him. Shakespeare's plays have been translated into every major existent language and are performed more often than those of any other playwright.

Katherine: She is the eldest daughter of Baptista and sister to Bianca. She is extremely strong willed and likes to say what she thinks and how she feels. She is often abusive and angry, but she is mellowed by Petruchio.

Petruchio: He is wealthy, eccentric, loud, and rude. He has come to Padua to marry a wealthy woman. He decides to marry Katherine and turn her into an obedient, caring wife.

Baptista: He is a wealthy man of Padua. He has two daughters he adores, Katherine and Bianca, on whom he lavishes his wealth. However, he is unsure how to handle the strong-willed Katherine.

The Taming of the Shrew

Katherine was the eldest daughter of Baptista, a wealthy merchant in the city of Padua, Italy. Katherine was well known in the town, but entirely

for the wrong reasons.
She was considered the
foulest-tempered woman
in the whole of Padua,
and according to some,
even beyond. She would
start screaming at people
for no reason, causing
her father a great deal of
embarrassment on account
of her behavior. Such was
her unpopularity in the
town that she was known
as Katherine the Shrew.

But Baptista's greatest
problem with Katherine
was something else.
Every day, Baptista would
receive offers of marriage

from gallant and noble men
from Padua and neighboring
towns, but for his younger
daughter Bianca, not Katherine.
However, he had to send them
away, claiming that until he
could find someone to marry
Katherine, how could he even

think about Bianca? So, poor Bianca had to remain unmarried because of her sister.

At that time, a young man had arrived in the city. His name was Petruchio and his purpose for coming to Padua was simple—to find a bride. He had heard about Katherine and, surprisingly, had decided to take her as his wife. He had heard that she was rich and also very pretty. He claimed that in time he would turn her into a meek and obedient wife.

Now Petruchio was
naturally a good-tempered
man, but he could also get angry
enough to kill someone. And

so, bearing this in mind, he knew that he would be able to change Katherine's nature.

Petruchio soon put his plan to woo Katherine into action. He first went to her father, Baptista, and said that he wanted his permission to ask for his gentle daughter's hand in marriage. Baptista was shocked to hear someone call Katherine gentle, though he was happy that someone actually wanted to marry her. Just as Baptista was about to reply, Katherine's music teacher came

barging into the room, crying
in pain. He complained that
when he had pointed out
some flaws in Katherine's lute
playing, she broke the very
same lute over his head!

When Petruchio heard the
story, he laughed loudly and
claimed that the pretty Katherine

was just a child and he loved
her even more after hearing of
her antics. He said he needed
Baptista's consent to marriage
immediately, for he was in a great
hurry. His father had
recently died, leaving
him with all his
lands and money.

He also wanted to know that in
the event he married Katherine,
what Baptista would give as
a dowry. Baptista knew this
was a little unusual for a lover,
but he was so overjoyed at the
thought of seeing Katherine
married that he promised to
give twenty thousand crowns

and half of his estate at the time of his death as a dowry. Satisfied, Petruchio immediately wanted to see his bride-to-be.

As Baptista went indoors to find Katherine, the good-tempered youth started to plan his courtship strategy to tame the shrew. He said to himself,

"I will win her with spirit when she comes. If she shouts at me, then I will tell her she sings as sweetly as a nightingale; and if she frowns, I will say she looks as beautiful as roses newly washed with dew; if she does not speak a word, I will praise the eloquence of her language; and if she bids me to leave her,

I will thank her as if she bid me to stay for a week." Petruchio knew that he must get the better of Katherine at all costs.

As soon as Katherine came before him, Petruchio put his plan into action. He started by

calling her Kate. Obviously,
Katherine was in no mood
to be befriended at that time
and she reminded him that
her name was Katherine. But
Petruchio was not one to be
stopped so easily. He continued
to call her Kate and said she

was the prettiest Kate in the world. He claimed that he had heard about her mildness being praised in every town and had therefore come to ask for her hand in marriage.

Katherine was completely dazed and had heard enough. Soon, she was displaying to

Petruchio the very behavior
that was the reason she was
known as Katherine the Shrew.
But the more she tried to insult
Petruchio, the more he continued
to praise her. When Petruchio
heard Baptista approaching, to
keep the charade going he loudly
informed Katherine that they

had had enough idle talk and
that he was going to marry her
soon, as he had already discussed
the matter with her father.

As soon as Baptista came
before them, Petruchio informed
him how sweetly Katherine
had greeted him and that she
had agreed to marry him next

Sunday. Katherine was shocked
by this comment and declared
that she would rather see him
hanged the next Sunday. But
Petruchio merely shrugged it
off, telling Baptista that she
had said they would pretend
not to be getting married. He
then informed Katherine and
her father that he would go
and purchase the finest clothes

for his beloved Katherine to
wear, and would be back on
Sunday for the wedding.

However, on Sunday, when
all the guests arrived for the

wedding, Petruchio was nowhere to be found. Katherine began to think that he had just made a fool of her and she was, as usual, fuming. But at last Petruchio arrived—only he was dressed in strange, untidy clothes, far from what a bridegroom would be

expected to wear. Even his
horse and servant who had
accompanied him on the
journey looked peculiar.

Though everyone
present tried to get him
to change into something
more appropriate for
a wedding, Petruchio
could not be convinced
and continued to behave
rather oddly. When the
priest asked him if he
would take Katherine
as his wife, he started
swearing at the top of his
voice, causing the priest
to drop his book. As the
priest tried to retrieve

it, Petruchio purposely tripped
him up, causing him to fall
off the altar. His actions were
so insane that even the foul
Katherine started to feel scared.

After the wedding, Petruchio
shouted at the waiter to get him
some wine and then started
drinking like a fish. Never had

there been a marriage like it in
the whole of Padua—or perhaps
even in the whole of Italy. But
Petruchio knew what he was

doing. This was perhaps his only chance to tame his shrewish wife.

Baptista had arranged for a grand feast to celebrate the marriage of his daughter. But Petruchio decided to go back to his own house with his wife, Katherine, immediately.

Baptista tried to reason with
him, and Katherine of course
gave him a mouthful, but as had
been happening all morning,
nothing could convince
Petruchio. He said that as her
husband, he now had control
over her and that he would do

as he pleased. So strange were his antics that no one present even tried to stop him.

The horse that he had brought with him for Katherine to ride was another odd sight, as it looked as if the poor beast would be unable to carry even a small child. But Petruchio placed

Katherine on the horse and, mounting a similar-looking horse himself, they set off immediately.

After a long, long journey, they finally reached their destination. But Petruchio's crazy actions would not cease. He asked his servants to serve dinner immediately. But when

the food arrived, he started
throwing everything around,
exclaiming that nothing on the
table was fit for his lovely wife.

Tired and starved, Katherine
decided to go to sleep, but
even then her husband had to
interfere, throwing pillows and
mattresses off the bed, claiming
that the servants had not made
the bed well enough for her
to sleep in. Poor Katherine
tried to doze off on a chair, but

Petruchio's constant ramblings kept her awake all night.

The next day was no different. Petruchio started by throwing the breakfast away, claiming that the servants had not made it well. How could he feed that to his beloved wife? The haughty Katherine, who would never listen to others or speak a kind word, started to beg the servants for

some food. But the servants had
been instructed by their master
not to give her anything. They
were helpless. Poor Katherine

did not know what to do. She could not understand what she needed to do to get some food and some sleep. And the worst part was that her husband did all this in the name of pure love.

Finally, Petruchio walked into the room with a small helping of meat, claiming that he had cooked it himself for his dear wife. All he wanted in return was a thank-you. But Katherine did not know how to say that

phrase, for she had never used it in her life. Since she would not thank him for bringing the little piece of meat, Petruchio thought that she was not happy with it and wanted to throw it away. Unable to see more food being taken away from her on flimsy excuses, Katherine finally said, "Thank you!"

As she fell ravenously on the small meal that had been

provided, Petruchio told her
that they would now return to
her father's house and rejoin
the celebrations. To prove that
he was speaking the truth, he
asked his servant to bring in
all the clothes that he had had
made for her. However, he was

not happy with the bonnet, as he thought it very small. But Katherine, between bites, said, "I will have this. All gentlewomen wear such bonnets as these." But Petruchio's prompt response was, "When you are gentle you shall wear one too, and not till then."

But by now the meal had revived Katherine to some extent and she was back to her old tantrums. She immediately reminded Petruchio that she was going to speak her mind, whether he liked it or not. After all, his betters had always listened

to her and therefore so should he. But this was obviously not going to work with Petruchio.

He first turned the matter away from the bonnet and started finding faults with the design of the gown, though Katherine

felt it was one of the best gowns
she had ever seen. Hearing this,
Petruchio started scolding the
dressmakers who had made
the clothes for Katherine,
driving them away from the
hall. He then told Katherine
that they would leave for her
father's house in what they were

wearing and arrive there by
seven in the evening. But since
it was already past two in the
afternoon, Katherine advised
him that they would not be
able to arrive by suppertime.
But obviously, Petruchio was
not going to back down.

He kept up his madness throughout most of the journey, claiming that he was the sun god and his word was final. When Katherine did not agree, they turned back. He had made up his mind that he would not let her return to her father's house until she was completely calm. Over the next few days, they

tried to make several visits to
Padua and to Baptista's house,
but each time they had to come
back midway, because Katherine
would not call the moon the
sun as her husband did.

Finally, one day, the couple
was able to get nearer to Padua

than before, because Katherine
started to agree with whatever
her husband said. He called the
sun the moon, and without even
batting an eyelid she agreed.
That day, when Petruchio met
an old man on the road, he
decided to set another test for

his wife. He hailed the old man as a young maiden and ordered his wife to hail him in the same way. Without even turning her head, Katherine addressed the old man as a beautiful maiden,

whose beauty had completely
captured her heart. But Petruchio
was quick to test her again by
asking her how she could call
this old man a beautiful maiden.
Katherine, with her newfound

obedience, started to address
the man as the old man he
really was, blaming the sun for
playing tricks on her eyes.

Petruchio, now satisfied
with Katherine's temperament,
asked the old man who he was
and where he was heading. The

old traveler told them that his name was Vincentio. He was the father of Lucentio, a noble youth who was to be married to Baptista's younger daughter, Bianca, at Padua that day. Hearing the news, Petruchio offered that he should ride with

them, as they too were heading for Padua. When they finally arrived at Baptista's residence, he welcomed them heartily.

That evening, as the women retired to their chambers, both

Baptista and Lucentio started to
make fun of Petruchio and his
headstrong wife, Katherine the
Shrew. But Petruchio was
unfazed and challenged them
to a wager, declaring that his
wife was more obedient than
Bianca or any other woman
they could think of. Once the

wager was settled at one hundred crowns, Lucentio turned to a servant and said, "Please tell my wife that her husband entreats her to join him." But when the servant came back, he merely said that Bianca had refused to come and would rather have Lucentio join her in the parlor.

Though their own wives had not come, Lucentio and Baptista were sure that Katherine would never come to Petruchio. But Petruchio merely turned to the

servant and said, "Tell my wife that her husband commands her to come here immediately." And even before the servant returned, in came Katherine and asked her husband what she could do for him.

Baptista was amazed to see his daughter obediently listening to every word Petruchio said and obeying him without any retort. He told Petruchio that he would increase her dowry by another twenty thousand crowns, because the girl that stood before him was but another man's daughter.

Soon, Katherine was once again the most well-known girl in the whole of Padua—no longer as Katherine the Shrew, but as Katherine, the most obedient girl in the whole city, or perhaps in the whole of Italy.